A Note to Parents

DK READERS is a compelling program for beginning readers, designed in conjunction with leading literacy experts, including Dr. Linda Gambrell, Distinguished Professor of Education at Clemson University. Dr. Gambrell has served as President of the National Reading Conference, the College Reading Association, and the International Reading Association.

Beautiful illustrations and superb full-color photographs combine with engaging, easy-to-read stories to offer a fresh approach to each subject in the series. Each DK READER is guaranteed to capture a child's interest while developing his or her reading skills, general knowledge, and love of reading.

The five levels of DK READERS are aimed at different reading abilities, enabling you to choose the books that are exactly right for your child:

Pre-level 1: Learning to read
Level 1: Beginning to read
Level 2: Beginning to read alone
Level 3: Reading alone
Level 4: Proficient readers

The "normal" age at which a child begins to read can be anywhere from three to eight years old. Adult participation through the lower levels is very helpful for providing encouragement, discussing storylines, and sounding out unfamiliar words.

No matter which level you select, you can be sure that you are helping your child learn to read, then read to learn!

LONDON, NEW YORK, MUNICH,
MELBOURNE, and DELHI

Editor Shari Last
Designer Mark Richards
Jacket Designer Lauren Rosier
Design Manager Ron Stobbart
Publishing Manager Catherine Saunders
Art Director Lisa Lanzarini
Publisher Simon Beecroft
Publishing Director Alex Allan
Production Editor Marc Staples
Production Controller Melanie Mikellides
Reading Consultant Dr. Linda Gambrell

First published in the United States in 2012
by DK Publishing
375 Hudson Street
New York, New York 10014
10 9 8 7 6 5 4 3 2 1
LEGO and the LEGO Logo are trademarks of The LEGO Group.
Copyright © 2012 The LEGO Group.
Produced by Dorling Kindersley
under license from The LEGO Group.

001—183089—May/12

DK books are available at special discounts when purchased in bulk
for sales promotions, premiums, fund-raising, or educational use.
For details, contact:
DK Publishing Special Markets
375 Hudson Street
New York, New York 10014
SpecialSales@dk.com

A catalog record for this book is available
from the Library of Congress.

ISBN: 978-0-7566-9005-2 (Paperback)
ISBN: 978-0-7566-9006-9 (Hardcover)

Color reproduction by Media Development and Printing, UK
Printed and bound in the USA by Lake Book Manufacturing, Inc.

Discover more at
www.dk.com
www.LEGO.com

Contents

LEGO HERO FACTORY

MEET THE HEROES

Written by Shari Last

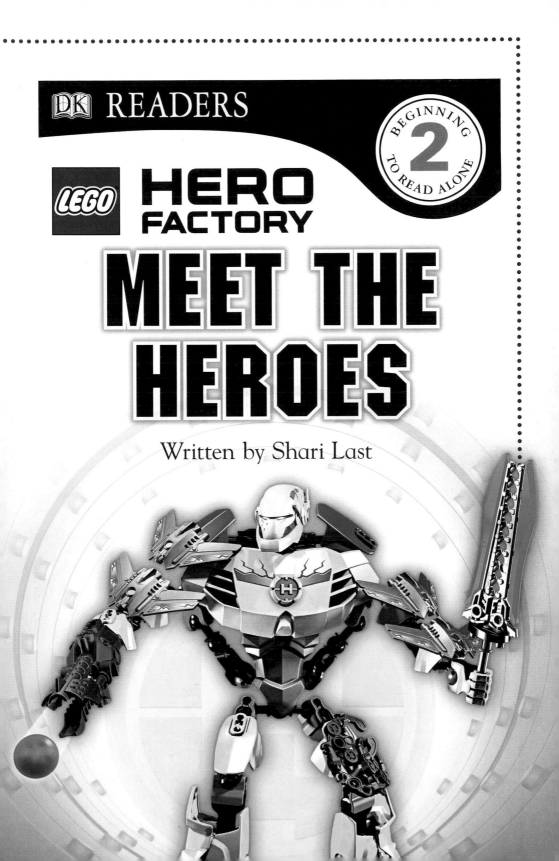

Makuhero City

Welcome to Makuhero City, home of the brave robot heroes. The heroes are built at the Hero Factory—the tallest and most famous building in the city.

Mr. Makuro
Mr. Makuro is the founder of the Hero Factory and the chief robot designer. He is very old and wise.

apartment building

Millions of robots live in Makuhero City, including the heroes. They are always ready for their next exciting mission!

Hero Factory

Building a Hero

Every day the Hero Factory produces new heroes. First a robot body is designed and built. Then a Hero Core is placed inside the body… and it comes to life! A new hero is called a rookie. He or she still has a lot to learn. After many hours of difficult training, the rookie becomes a full hero…

Hero Core
The Hero Core is made from a special rock called Quaza. Quaza is rare and very precious.

…Now he or she is ready to go on a real mission.

The Heroes

The heroes have an important job to do. They protect the universe from dangerous villains and go on exciting missions to other planets.

The heroes solve mysteries, capture villains, and save people from danger. It is a tough job being a hero, but these robots are proud to do it! Now let's meet some of the brave heroes.

Preston Stormer

Preston Stormer is the most famous hero in Makuhero City.

Brave Stormer has captured hundreds of villains and saved hundreds of people! He never gets scared on a mission—even when it looks dangerous.

Stormer is the leader of Team Alpha, an elite group of heroes who go on missions together.

Ultramach speedcycle
Stormer has an Ultramach speedcycle. Here, he rides this speedy bike as he chases the villain Speeda Demon.

Rocka

Rocka is a new member of Team Alpha. He sometimes acts without thinking, which can get him into trouble. However, he also possesses secret intelligence skills, which he will soon reveal…

hero cuffs

crossbow

energy
shield

Rocka wields a weapon called a
crossbow, which shoots deadly
arrows. It looks so scary that his
enemies keep their distance!

Jimi Stringer

Hero Jimi Stringer is a member of Team Alpha. He can control sound waves using his sound blaster weapon. It knocks his enemies over with a powerful blast of sound!

A confident hero

Stringer is confident enough to go on a mission on his own. He travels to the planet Tansari IV to capture the villain Voltix.

Stringer is a calm, friendly hero who is always happy to help rookies with their training.

hero cuffs

sound blaster

plasma
gun

Mark Surge

Mark Surge is the youngest
member of Team Alpha. He is
energetic and unpredictable.

Although he is still a rookie, Surge has learnt a lot from Preston Stormer and the rest of Team Alpha. He is bold in battle and always ready for action—especially when he wields his powerful Electricity shooter. Villains beware!

Electricity shooter

Natalie Breez

Natalie Breez is another rookie member of Team Alpha. She is very clever and is good at getting out of tricky situations.

Breez can move as fast as the wind thanks to the high-tech rocket boots she wears. She also carries a Hex energy shield. This big red shield bounces bullets or plasma blasts back at whoever shoots at her!

Breez is full of energy and she can't wait for her next mission… so the villains better watch out!

Hex energy
shield

rocket
boots

William Furno

William Furno might be a rookie, but he's very confident.

Aquajet pack

plasma gun

He looks up to his team leader, Stormer, who often gives him advice. Furno is well-equipped for underwater battles. He has an Aquajet pack to propel him through water, and a plasma gun for capturing fish-like villains, such as Jawblade!

Speeder bike
When Furno battles on land, he has a superfast speeder bike to help him catch up with the villains.

plasma
shooter

Nathan Evo

Nathan Evo is the newest rookie
to join Team Alpha. He is
enthusiastic and fearless.

Evo has been programmed to communicate with almost any machine. His body has been fitted with a sturdy tank arm. It can fire a powerful plasma shooter and smash through any obstacles in Evo's path.

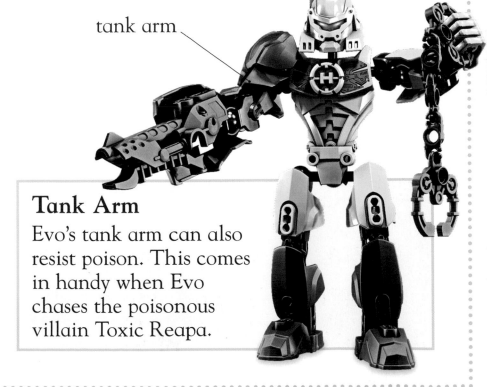

tank arm

Tank Arm
Evo's tank arm can also resist poison. This comes in handy when Evo chases the poisonous villain Toxic Reapa.

Dunkan Bulk

Dunkan Bulk is one of the most experienced heroes on Team Alpha. He is big and bulky, just like his name!

Bulk can be very clumsy and is always bumping into things. Maybe this is because of how big he is. Or because he usually acts first and thinks later! Bulk might not be the smartest hero in Team Alpha, but he is one of the strongest and bravest heroes in all of Makuhero City.

Julius Nex

Julius Nex is a hero you can trust. He is both tough and flexible, which means he can take on more than one villain at a time.

hero cuffs

precision
laser
cutters

Nex is an important member
of Team Alpha. All the other
heroes feel better when he
is around. And the villains?
Well, they start to feel a bit
worried when Nex shows up…

Villains

The heroes would love to relax with their friends all day. Unfortunately, there are many villains on the loose, and it is up to the heroes to catch them.

Black Phantom

Toxic Reapa

Toxic Reapa fires deadly poison. **Black Phantom** is enormous and very powerful. **Core Hunter** has scary spikes on his back. **Jawblade** is quick as a shark underwater. **Splitface** is as mad as he is dangerous.

Jawblade

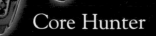

Core Hunter

Splitface

Thornraxx can fly. Watch out for his poisonous sting. **XT4** has four arms, which means he can wield four weapons at once! **Speeda Demon** is almost too fast to catch.

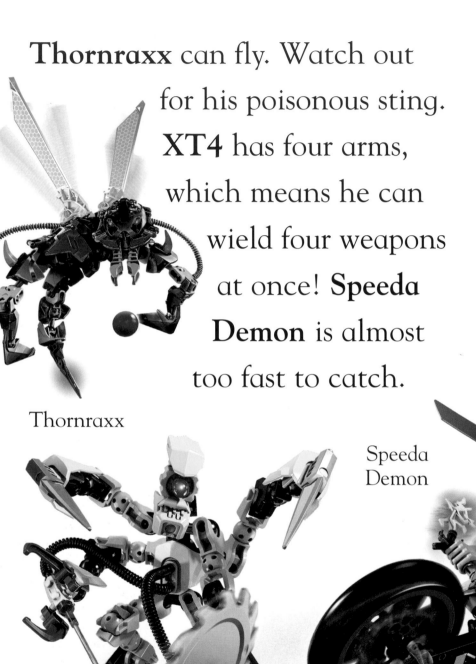

Thornraxx

Speeda
Demon

XT4

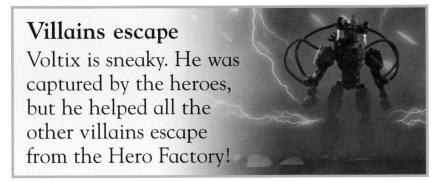

Voltix can control electricity, so
his attacks are usually shocking.
Can the robot heroes defeat
these terrible foes?

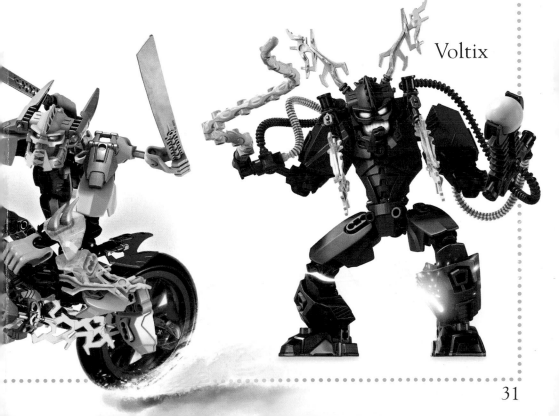

Voltix

Quiz!

1. Where do the robot heroes live?

2. Who is the leader of Team Alpha?

3. Which hero can control sound?

4. What is a Hero Core made from?

5. Which villain has the body of a shark?

Answers: 1. Makuhero City 2. Stormer 3. Stringer 4. Quaza rock 5. Jawblade